Sink or Swim

For Mark, Dan and Will - DT

First published 2008
Evans Brothers Limited
2A Portman Mansions
Chiltern Street
London W1U 6NR

British Library Cataloguing in Publication Data

Taylor, Dereen
    Sink or swim. - (Spirals)
    1. Children's stories
    I. Title
    823.9'2[J]

ISBN-13: 978 0 237 53531 5 (hb)
ISBN-13: 978 0 237 53535 3 (pb)

Printed in China

Editor: Louise John
Design: Robert Walster
Production: Jenny Mulvanny

Sink or Swim

Dereen Taylor
and Marijke van Veldhoven

William's big sister is called Hattie.
William loves Hattie. Most of the time.

Hattie is really good at climbing trees and making people laugh. Hattie never, ever stops talking.

Mum asks Hattie and William what they would like for tea.

Hattie says, "Fish fingers and chips, please!"

Mum asks how many fish fingers they would like.

Hattie says, "Three each, please. With lots of ketchup!"

Dad asks Hattie and William what TV programme they would like to watch.

Hattie says, "The one about the ballerina sleepover!"

William thinks ballerinas are really boring. His favourite programme is the one about the dragon with bad breath.

Hattie and William play in the garden with their next-door neighbours, Jess and Tom.

"Let's play pirates!" says Hattie.

Jess and Tom shout and laugh as they chase after Captain Hattie.

William really wanted to play secret agents.

Hattie tells Nana and Grandad she saw a squirrel swinging on the washing line in the garden.

Nana and Grandad laugh.

William wants to make Nana and Grandad laugh, too. But he can't think of any funny jokes or stories.

13

Hattie and William are moving up from the junior pool to the big pool for their swimming lessons. Hattie is very excited.

She talks about her new stripey swimming costume.

She talks about breaststroke and backstroke.

She talks about being a really good swimmer and going snorkelling in the sea on holiday.

William listens. He doesn't say anything. He's feeling worried about swimming in the big pool.

Ben Foster said that his cousin once sank in the deep end.

William won't be able to touch the bottom. And he doesn't want to sink like Ben Foster's cousin.

On the way to swimming, Hattie makes
up a funny rhyme:

I have just one wish
To swim like a fish
Why do you think?
So I don't sink!

Mum laughs.
William just hopes he doesn't sink.

Hattie chats to an older girl in the changing room. Hattie's new friend is called Rose. She's been swimming in the big pool for ages.

William holds his goggles tight and tries not to worry.

Hattie and William's new swimming teacher is called Miss Bream.

She tells them that, just like in the junior pool, the most important thing they have to do in their swimming lesson is listen.

William feels a bit better. He's good at listening.

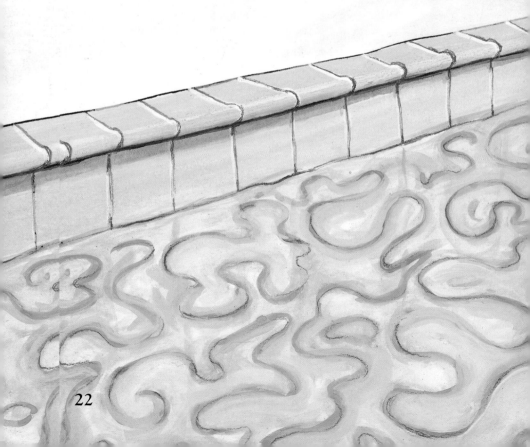

In the water, Miss Bream asks Hattie and Rose to stop talking.

William can't touch the bottom. But he enjoys the feel of the water swishing between his toes. He wiggles his legs gently as he listens to what Miss Bream is saying.

Miss Bream asks the children to take turns swimming across the width of the pool.

William is glad he doesn't have to go first.

Hattie is still chatting to Rose when she puts her face in the water and pushes off from the side.

Now it's William's turn. He can feel butterflies turning somersaults in his tummy. He takes a deep breath, puts his head under the water and opens his eyes.

The water is very deep – but really peaceful. William swims across to the other side.

On the way home Hattie is quiet. She's not sure at all about swimming lessons in the big pool. There's too much listening. And too much water in your mouth.

William says, "Guess what, Mum? I didn't sink!"

Why not try reading another **Spirals** book?

Megan's Tick Tock Rocket by Andrew Fusek Peters,
Polly Peters and Simona Dimitri
ISBN 978 0237 53348 9 (hb)
ISBN 978 0237 53342 7 (pb)

Growl! by Vivian French and Tim Archbold
ISBN 978 0237 53351 9 (hb)
ISBN 978 0237 53345 8 (pb)

John and the River Monster by Paul Harrison and
Ian Benfold Haywood
ISBN 978 0237 53350 2 (hb)
ISBN 978 0237 53344 1 (pb)

Froggy Went a Hopping by Alan Durant and Sue Mason
ISBN 978 0237 53352 6 (hb)
ISBN 978 0237 53346 5 (pb)

Amy's Slippers by Mary Chapman and Simona Dimitri
ISBN 978 0237 53353 3 (hb)
ISBN 978 0237 53347 2 (pb)

The Flamingo Who Forgot by Alan Durant and Franco Rivolli
ISBN 978 0237 53349 6 (hb)
ISBN 978 0237 53343 4 (pb)

Glub! by Penny Little and Sue Mason
ISBN 978 0237 53462 2 (hb)
ISBN 978 0237 53461 5 (pb)

The Grumpy Queen by Valerie Wilding and Simona Sanfilippo
ISBN 978 0237 53460 8 (hb)
ISBN 978 0237 53459 2 (pb)

Happy by Mara Bergman and Simona Sanfilippo
ISBN 978 0237 53532 2 (hb)
ISBN 978 0237 53536 0 (pb)

Sink or Swim by Dereen Taylor and Marijke van Veldhoven
ISBN 978 0237 53531 5 (hb)
ISBN 978 0237 53535 3 (pb)

Sophie's Timepiece by Mary Chapman and Nigel Baines
ISBN 978 0237 53530 8 (hb)
ISBN 978 0237 53534 6 (pb)